AF207387

The Man Who Learned to Walk In Shoes That Pinch

For Pia —

May you NEVER walk in shoes that pinch!

Best wishes —
Margaret Harmon

The Man Who Learned to Walk In Shoes That Pinch

**Contemporary Fables by
Margaret Harmon**

Abyss Publications
San Diego

Library of Congress Catalog Card Number 92-72656

ISBN 0-9628423-1-1

Manufactured in the United States of America.
First Edition.

"The Woman, the Boyfriend, and the Car" appeared in *The Cowles Mountain Journal*. "The Toad Who Knew It All" aired on KPBS Radio San Diego's *San Diego Journal* and the *Journal*'s *Retrospective: Best Writers in San Diego*.

For Wayne,
Andrea, and Fritz

Acknowledgements

Many talented people have contributed generously to this book. Editors Bette Pegas and Dorothy Ledbetter, and test readers Ann Sensibaugh, Bertha and Nelson Fuller, Ed Fuller, Andrea Harmon, Fritz Harmon, Faye Girsch, Joy McAllister, Greta Ross, Jane Keller, Ann Wolfensberger, Martha Thomas, Claudette de Courley, Martha Sosey, Robert Lawrence, Maxine Seltzer, Dennis Miley, and Ruth Unterman were perceptive, articulate, and supportive. Natasha Josefowitz gave unique professional assistance, and Charles Harrington Elster put PINCH fables on public radio. Wayne Harmon's humor and support were indispensable. I'm grateful for the skills and steadfastness of publisher Ralph Cates and book designer Cheryl Solheid, and for Brian Staples' and Jeannie Ledbetter's technical assistance.

The Santa Barbara Writers' Conference's extraordinary staff—especially Shelly Lowenkopf, Ian Bernard, Barnaby Conrad, Ray Bradbury, and Jonathan Winters—and astute conferees helped shape these fables and their path to publication.

Preface

I love fables. They help us make our lives work: achieve selfhood, be healthy, give and receive love, make our fortune, see life realistically, steward the earth. We joke in fables, but only on serious topics.

I like the clarity of fables in a murky world. Heroes and villains alike live by their principles—you sail the boat you build.

It's each fable's purpose, of course, to examine one virtue, vice, or attitude by personifying it in a character who never abandons it, though sorely tested—so we can see the consequences of shaping our own lives by that governing principle, without gambling our lives in the experiment.

Ah, the nobly wretched King Midas! He couldn't squash an ant and notice that his touch turned animals, too, to gold, and yell to the queen to keep their daughter out of the throne room until he could reverse his blessing-turned-curse. Midas was doomed to carry greed to its logical extreme—risking his daughter to save ours.

I admire fables' efficiency. No doubt fables have survived so long as a literary form because a fable communicates an idea as fully developed as an essay's, but in a form that allows to remember its message long after we've forgotten an essay's point. We retain fables' lessons because we experience them through our own senses. We hear the grasshopper fiddle and see the sweaty, muttering ants drag seeds up their hill. When Midas hugs his daughter, her body stiffens and cools into gold in our arms. We live a fable and merely read an essay.

It's fun to debate the meaning of a fable. Though we all read the same words, we each read our own fable—sort of a literary Rorschach. As we mature, fables mature with us; we see what we're capable of seeing. A vivid character breathes our air.

Fiction is the intellectual equivalent of dreams: characters speak in more than words; events have meaning beyond their plotted purpose. This is especially true of fables because their richly spare, stylized language pulls toward consciousness the essentials of life to which fables connect us.

It's comforting to watch good guys win and bad guys lose in fables. The cheerful peasant who plants his potatoes and saves his coins always ends up buying the farm of the whiny peasant who won't get dirt under his fingernails. Fables are fair because life tends to be fair, if we wait long enough—and because we have to live as though it is. Catastrophes and injustice occur in fables, as in life, but the cheerful clever peasant overcomes even catastrophe and injustice better than the whiny peasant.

These fables are longer and more complex than Aesop's because our lives are longer and more complex than his. Besides, the short, easy fables have already been done.

The PINCH fables don't have pithy little morals written at their ends because a single sentence doesn't capture a complex fable. Without a short moral, we think of the whole fable, with its shades and layers of meaning to us.

I love the intimacy of fables. A fable is a metaphor we each use in infinite private variety—comforting, straightening, sustaining, renewing the self we shape.

Fables are a wonderful literary form.

Contents

The
Woman,
the
Boyfriend,
and the
Car

There was once a young woman named Sylvia who went out on her own. She found a job and bought a small car that got forty-two miles per gallon, in town.

She saved her money and went to a shopping center to buy new clothes: a ruffly blouse, full gored skirt, high-heeled shoes, and delicate gold jewelry that made her feel feminine and slender. She curled her hair in golden honey ringlets that tumbled to her shoulders. To the office, she wore shirtwaist dresses that emphasized her wholesomeness. Sylvia felt sweet.

Stanley, a man in the office, thought she looked

sweet, too. He asked her to dinner. Then to dance. Then to a play, an excellent dinner, and to bed, to bed, to bed. He asked her to marry him. She accepted.

As Sylvia showed her substantial engagement ring around the office, some women executives asked if she'd moved into Stanley's apartment. When Sylvia said no, they said that was a mistake. Marriage was forever, almost, and it was necessary to check out every variable in a relationship. One of them commented that she was out of it, anyway, with her modelly good looks, excessive femininity, and letting Stanley drive her to work in his car. It was offending a lot of women in the office who'd fought hard for equal rights and pay. Didn't she care anything for her sisters?

Sylvia thought it over. She had her hair cut short and frizzed. She moved in with Stanley and paid half the rent and food and refused to wash dishes unless he made the bed and folded laundry. They both burned the food or ate out. They took turns driving to work.

She pushed her shirtwaist dresses to the end of the closet and bought some blazers and tweedy knits. Crepe-soled shoes made her feel a little cubic, but they were certainly easy to walk in.

Stanley said it had been an excellent idea to live together; he'd discovered she wasn't anything like what he'd thought when he bought the ring. He demanded it back and asked her to leave.

She said, "Great! There's no way I can keep both my career and your childish needs covered in a twenty-four-hour day. I want my freedom back."

She moved into a new apartment and decorated the walls with blown-up posters of feminists who'd climbed to the top of the corporate ladder. She poured her guts into her work and built a reputation for ferocity and cleverness. She beat every deadline and humiliated all opponents. She bought a red Alfa Romeo.

One day, in a restroom cubicle, Sylvia heard voices come into the room hotly discussing somebody. "Butch!" someone spat. "You heard why Stanley broke up with her, didn't you? He found out she was gay, and refused to cover for her. She dresses like a man, thinks like a man, works like a man. I bet when she comes in here she stands up."

"Well, she's making a wad of money now, with that promotion. I just wonder who she spends it on. She can't date in public, and keep her job with old Mr. Wilson. It must kill her to have to sneak."

Someone ran water and somebody else flushed a toilet. Sylvia pulled her feet up so no one would recognize her shoes.

The voices left the restroom, and hissed off down the corridor. Sylvia waited awhile before she left her cubicle and looked in the mirror.

Her hair had been getting shorter and shorter. She was wearing platinum post earrings, a tank watch, and a dark gray flannel suit with a precise pinstripe. Between her unmascaraed eyes were two unmistakable fierceness-furrows. Sylvia stepped back and stared at her reflection.

That afternoon she left work early to go to a high-fashion boutique with flashing stagelights. Sylvia bought a mauve satin wrap-around dress, ultra-high ankle-strap shoes, a feather boa, and textured hose. In a drugstore she bought Vogue and Harper's Bazaar and all the makeup they mentioned by name.

She spent the rest of the evening in the bathroom, experimenting with her face, imitating the makeup on the models in the ads and articles. By nine o'clock her face was so sore she had to bite a washcloth while she rubbed cold cream into her cheeks to remove the last makeup job of the night. She soaked her hair in a hot shower, to make it grow.

The next day she drove to work with the top down on the Alfa. She wore the mauve dress, ankle-strap shoes, new makeup, and her hair moussed for volume. Her earrings were so large they snagged the satin shoulders of her dress.

"Slut!" she heard at the water cooler.

"Trampy woman," was muttered to her in the elevator.

"Cheezuss!" was the reaction of her department's legal adviser.

Mr. Wilson, senior, buzzed her into his office after lunch. "We have an image here at Wilson, Wilson, Wilson, and Sons," he said. "If people are to entrust their fortunes to us, we must look fortunate. They have to believe we will know how to handle their money. In that outfit, you look as though you're in the process of procuring yours, by unsavory means. We communicate as much through our clothing as through our words. I suggest that you leave this building by the back elevator and not return until you look like a Wilson person."

Sylvia left the office, raised the top on her car, and drove to a mall, where she bought five pastel wool Evan Picone suits (fitted loosely across the derrière and bust), seven coordinated silk blouses, a cashmere sweater set, and a string of pearls. She gratefully exchanged her ankle-straps for French leather pumps with tiny tassels and bought a matching brown leather handbag.

She left her Alfa Romeo at a body shop, to be painted black and have its red upholstery covered with neutral brown fabric. She opened a separate money market account to save for a beige Mercedes sedan.

Mr. Wilson smiled at her in the hall the next day, but the young secretaries began treating her like their mothers. They asked her advice on fiftieth wedding anniversary presents and for older people's political views. Men stopped flirting with her, and she was never asked for identification, in even the darkest cocktail lounge. Her mail started coming addressed to Mrs. . . . . Finally, one day several months later, she heard a messenger directing someone to her as "the matronly woman there with her hair in a bun."

Sylvia stared at the messenger and then at her reflection in the glassed lithograph on her office wall. She snapped off her computer, without saving the file, and walked into Mr. Wilson's office unannounced. Sylvia demanded her paycheck, money for six weeks of accumulated vacation, and her funds from the company savings plan. "I'm quitting," she said.

Mr. Wilson, shocked, begged her to reconsider. But he stopped when she untied the bow on her blouse and stepped out of her shoes, one by one, deliberately. When she shook the bobby pins from her hair and started unbuttoning her blouse, he grabbed his fountain pen and wrote a voucher for fifty-four thousand five hundred dollars and hustled her out of his office.

Sylvia didn't bother to clean out her desk at WVI. She drove straight to a nudist colony on the Mexican border and checked everything, including her earrings, in the colony safe. She lived there for several months with a Mr. Universe contender who had a year-round tan even on the bottom of his tongue. She sold her car and became a lacto-ovo vegetarian.

But when Sylvia failed to send out Christmas cards, her mother flew to the nudist colony to see if she was all right. It was not a good visit.

"Sylvia! What would your father say? Put your clothes on this instant and come back to Cincinnati."

"Mother," Sylvia protested, "we haven't lived

in Cincinnati since I was seven."

"And that's the last time you made sense to me. You'll either catch your death of cold or get skin cancer from all this sun. Put your clothes on, right now."

Sylvia got her clothes from the colony safe, rode back to her old apartment with her mother, and promised to get a job and wear clothes. Her mother flew home, but called every week.

Sylvia's awareness of her physical self had been awakened during her months in the nudist colony, and she decided to work in a bicycle shop and wear lycra cycling tights and tank tops, without underwear. She wore cleats without socks, too. Her hair grew long and she affected a sun visor, even indoors. She kept her tan up, oiled her body, and cycled fifty miles a day. She let the bike shop owner move into her apartment because he couldn't afford to run the shop at a loss and still pay for a place to live.

One day, while stopping for liquids in a park during one of her rides the length of California over a four-day weekend, Sylvia met two bearded philosophers. They were wearing long beaded caftans over leather trousers, and sandals that had grown to fit their feet in shape and smell.

Their hair was long and snarled, partly braided, partly curled. They were traveling across the country to explain the universe to the American public. At the moment they were collecting aluminum cans in order to buy something to eat.

One of the philosophers said to Sylvia, "You obviously expend all your consciousness on your physical body. You must develop your mind. I see that you have no white at all in your aura." He felt her thigh critically. "You can't build muscle like this without pouring sixteen hours a day into it. What time does that leave for your soul?" He shook his head.

The other philosopher added, "You're the most grossly out of balance person I've seen in eighteen states." He choked back tears, but couldn't keep his lips from trembling.

Sylvia thought awhile, because this was a major decision. After considering all the pros and cons, she gave the philosophers her money and address and told them to take the bus to her apartment. She'd cycle there. They would become her private tutors until she balanced her life.

Back at the apartment, Sylvia kicked the cycle shop owner out and quit her job. She pressed her sports clothes into her closet to make room for caftans and leather vests and pants. There was barely room in the closet because during her sports phase she'd bought down-filled ski clothes. And she still had her ruffly clothes from her days with Stanley, her blazers and tweeds from her career-first era, her satin clothes from the boutique, and her Evan Picone suits and cashmeres from her Wilson person period. She still had her muscles, though, and she mashed the clothes into the closet until the clothes pole groaned and the hangers gnashed and sparked.

The philosophers moved into the apartment and taught Sylvia to live a simple, filthy life of contemplation and rhetoric. They read Hindu texts in the original Sanskrit, to purify the mind by intoning sounds without perceived meaning. They ate seeds, nuts, and raw vegetables. The last of Sylvia's money bought new beaded caftans and heavy cloaks of monkey skin and owl feathers. They walked everywhere, eschewing cars as a primary evil of the Western World. Anyway, cloaks are more dramatic when the wearer walks, or turns in place.

Sylvia learned to help stabilize the universe by collecting aluminum cans, returnable bottles, and newspapers. It provided enough money for seeds and vegetables.

One morning about six o'clock, Sylvia's neighbors were awakened by a thunderous crash in her apartment. The two philosophers were seen running from the apartment in horror, and one long muffled moan escaped the apartment after them.

When the manager entered, he found tragedy. Sylvia was lying crushed on the floor of her closet, with one end of the clothes pole, split and splintered, through her temple. She expired before his eyes, clutching the tons of clothes that had fallen on her when the clothes pole broke.

The coroner ruled the death accidental and, after measuring the stresses on the pole, said he didn't see how it had lasted as long as it had. Sylvia must have been choosing her clothes for the day, to dress, when the clothes pole split, fell, and impaled her.

Sylvia died absolutely penniless, but the state estimated her clothes' value at two hundred thousand dollars and sold them at auction to pay for Sylvia's burial. Unfortunately, the clothes sold too well and the profit put her into the maximum tax bracket so that, after taxes, legal fees and court costs, there was no money to pay for her interment. Sylvia was buried as a pauper, with a debt of $536.17 permanently on her record.

Sylvia's soul was evidently not pleased with the resolution of her affairs because there have been, ever since, reports of a young woman's ghost wandering the cemetery. It's difficult to corroborate the stories because everyone describes the ghost differently. Some people see a young lady with long hair tumbling about her shoulders as she floats across the grass in a filmy dress; children say she rides among the headstones on a silver bicycle. Lovers report a totally nude ghost who sits on the hoods of parked cars. Mr. Wilson admits, under pressure, that Sylvia comes back to the office occasionally, in her favorite Evan Picone, pearls, and pumps. But he knows it's just her ghost because he can see right through her.

The Elephant
and the
Rhinoceros

A beautiful young elephant married a well-established rhinoceros. She did not believe rhinos were really so different from elephants. And, besides, she believed her love would make him more demonstrative and less rigid.

The rhinoceros, on the other hand, thought he would set an example for the elephant and she would gradually grow more constant. He thought it was largely environment that made elephants so emotional.

Their differences sparked a rather electric attraction between them, and the intensity of their own desires bonded them with the hot epoxy of shared ambition.

The elephant dreamed of being a great dancer. Certainly, she had the gifts; her magnificent carriage, supple trunk, expressive ears, and powerful legs set her apart. She lacked only the self-confidence to put her art above social delights and household chores. If her nest wasn't made, she couldn't practice. If friends invited her to the water hole during rehearsal hours, she succumbed to their entreaties. There was a perversity, a self-defeating side to her nature, that stood between her and greatness.

She admired the rhinoceros for his discipline and commitment to his goals. If he loved her, his greatest gifts to her would be discipline and commitment to her art. This was beyond his fortune, which the elephant pictured buying master classes, exotic costumes, and world tours. She could see him lovingly, but firmly, turning away friends during practice hours, protecting her from temptation until she honed her talents into the perfection that would bring her real happiness.

The rhinoceros did, indeed, love her. He loved her extraordinary poise and amazing delicacy. He loved her beauty and intoxicating unpredictability.

His own spirit seemed dull beside hers.

He knew exactly what he wanted—he'd always known. And he'd worked for it tirelessly, from before dawn till after dusk. He'd never spent, only earned; never played, only worked; never lived, only earned a living. Now that his fortune was amassed, he wanted to live the life he'd earned. He pictured his beloved elephant showing him the ways of water holes and romps through tall grass. Her beauty beside him would erase those doubts about himself—those fears of groups in unstructured social settings. His beloved would hostess dinner parties where he could sit at the head of an elegant table, surveying guests who'd come to befriend him, who would see him adored by a beautiful elephant. In her presence, the guests would not see his shyness, or hear the silence while he tried desperately to think of the witty replies that came so easily to his charming elephant. She would be his guide through the interpersonal labyrinth. If she loved him, she would turn him from a fat wallet into a whole being.

The honeymoon went fairly well. After all, the elephant decided, she couldn't expect herself to be disciplined in this once-in-a-lifetime situation. She would see the effects of her love when she returned to regular classes and rehearsals. The rhinoceros was too enchanted by living within his love's aura to notice whether he was growing witty or meeting new people. His only uneasiness was a haunting emptiness, a sense that he was forgetting something or that he wasn't doing what he was supposed to be doing.

Alone together at home, at last, they set out to carve their dreams in time, sweat, and decision. The elephant watched the rhinoceros for signs of love. How would he build her self-discipline? When would he deepen her commitment to the dance?

Their second day home, a friend of the elephant's stopped in to visit while the elephant was doing warm-ups at the barre, and the rhinoceros was watching. To the elephant's surprise, the rhinoceros led the friend into the rehearsal room and left. But she noticed a hurt expression on his face. He's hurt, she thought, that I care so little for my art that I talk to friends instead of practicing. He's right. So she told her friend, "Could you come back for lunch? I practice three hours every morning, and if I cool down now, I'll have to start over. I hope you understand." The friend agreed to lunch, and left.

The rhinoceros was, indeed, hurt. He was upset over sharing his beloved with someone else. But he knew that was ridiculously possessive, so he left the room to get control of his feelings.

The elephant practiced harder than she ever had in her life, secure in the love of her rhinoceros who was already strengthening her commitment to the dance. She hurried out to lunch with her friend and returned to find the rhinoceros pacing her practice studio, perspiring. "That was a long lunch," he said.

"It's true," the elephant answered. "I'll never be a dancer if I take three-hour lunches." And, to demonstrate to him her commitment, she put on a fresh leotard and tights to dance until dinner time.

The rhinoceros, wearied by his self-reproaching, sank to the floor and watched the elephant. Just being with her, he began to relax. Even if she wouldn't stop dancing and focus her attention on him, he noticed how lovingly she looked at him while she danced. He felt himself transformed by the music and his beloved's grace into a creature less gnawed by self-doubt.

Watching for the second hour, however, he felt resentment building. Every moment she was home she was dancing, and whenever friends came over, she laughed and talked with them and ignored him. Didn't she sense his loneliness, his desire to make friends with her by his side? She wasn't planning any parties that he knew of. Wasn't she his wife? He clenched his jaws and narrowed his eyes.

He watched the elephant practice, over and over, a turning leap—a *tour jeté*, she called it. It irritated him. He closed his eyes, and the emptiness returned. What a waste of time—watching a dancing elephant! He felt he was in the wrong place, missing something important. His life was slipping from him, as moments, one by one, returned to the center of the earth to be reused, given to other creatures living different lives. The rhinoceros felt unwholesome—the way he did after eating a whole cheesecake by himself, when his tongue was sore and his mind felt only disrespect for his body.

He got up from the floor and left the room. He went into his study and began reorganizing the books for one of his businesses. He ran his eyes over the little numbers, which nearly tasted sweet to him. They were soothing, yet exciting. He felt like himself again. He didn't come out of his study until dinner time.

The elephant was not surprised to see him leave the practice studio; she'd known something was bothering him. She hoped it wasn't her technique; she hoped he was planning a tour or concert for her. Surely he wasn't displeased with her work!

At dinner, the elephant's and the rhinoceros' eyes met across the table. But they didn't say anything about their unhappiness. They couldn't admit they might have made a mistake, marrying an elephant or a rhinoceros.

In the days that followed, the rhinoceros spent more and more time alone with his financial records, and he enlarged his fortune yet again. He felt like himself, at least. The elephant practiced alone for hours each day, with no proud rhinoceros watching. She danced alone for the beauty, and for power over her resentment that she worked so hard and the rhinoceros didn't care—didn't even notice how much better she'd become. She rewarded herself with little gatherings of old friends. She had them over in ones and twos to tea or dinner. They took walks and romped at the water hole. Of course, she always invited the rhinoceros, to be polite. He always came along, though he didn't seem to enjoy it much. Stiff and stodgy, he appeared to be forcing himself. Stay home, then, the elephant thought. Don't force yourself for my sake! But he always came along, silent, small-eyed, with his horn sticking up like a tooth in the wrong place.

The rhinoceros felt frantic at the outings, panicked that he'd humiliate himself—in front of his own elephant, now, as well as her guests. She was no longer the source of his comfort; she was another reason to be shy. She floated around flapping her enormous ears. But he forced himself, as much to show her as to grow, himself. He learned to speak to strangers, and eventually to laugh with them. Some he liked much better than others, counting them more as his guests than hers.

It went on for a year, this hostility. Then, two years. Of course, there were moments of softness every day. The elephant fanned the rhinoceros with her ears. And there were many little ways they pleased each other. The rhinoceros nuzzled the elephant's exquisitely sensitive trunk. They grew accustomed to each other and found things to enjoy. It was just the major pain that hurt them, their central disappointment and disillusion that festered hot before it turned to a cold hard tumor of encapsulated resentment that powered the elephant's discipline and the rhinoceros' poise.

One day, however, the elephant and the rhinoceros had had enough. It was a very hot day, and tempers don't keep well in the heat. "Why are you never pleased with me?" the elephant bellowed. "I am a thousand per cent improved, and you never notice!"

"Notice *what*?" the rhinoceros roared. "I'd like you to notice WHO! I am your husband, and you pay more attention to your *shoes* than you do to me. I've had to struggle alone to make friends with your friends. Love *me*, help ME!"

"I'll do it alone, then," the elephant said. "I am, anyway! Why do I need you?"

"I'm nicer to your friends than you are!" the rhino shouted. "You ignore us all, to do nothing but dance."

The elephant was utterly crushed. Her rhinoceros cared absolutely nothing for her dancing. It was all an illusion, a catastrophic mistake. She ran away and left the rhinoceros sneering after her, "Point your toes!"

In the days of disillusion that followed, they decided to divorce. Rhinoceroses and elephants are, after all, very different.

They started dividing the furniture. They took pictures from the walls, and books from the shelves. Some things were very difficult to separate. The elephant wept on the quilt she'd stitched for their bed. The rhinoceros couldn't look at their wedding photographs. But they wrenched themselves apart with their eyes shut tight to hold in their tears.

The elephant tried living without a table and chairs, and the rhinoceros tried to sleep on the couch instead of the bed. The elephant didn't mind eating standing up; but whenever she saw a table, she remembered all the dinner conversations, the little parties, and the laughter. The rhinoceros could buy a new bed, but it was tearing his heart out to think he would never again lie close to his beloved elephant.

Finally, the elephant couldn't stand it. She took the bed, wedding photos, china, and books all back to the rhinoceros. "I don't want any of these," she said. "They only remind me of you, and how empty I feel."

The rhinoceros choked up and couldn't speak. He simply hugged his beloved elephant, and wouldn't let her go.

The elephant mused at last from the tip of her trunk, "You did not make me committed to the dance—you didn't even want me to dance. I did it myself."

Then, words tumbled out of the rhinoceros. "I was angry when you didn't help me make friends. But having done it myself, I know they like me."

The elephant took a deep breath. "I learned about discipline, watching you work. I always admired your priorities—even when they kept you from me."

"I knew," the rhino said, "that dancing nour-ishes your grace and poise, even when I couldn't say it. And you did help me—by telling your stories and laughing the way you do."

The elephant exhaled and relaxed her trunk.

"I love you," the rhinoceros said, watching his words reflecting in the elephant's eye.

The elephant wrapped her trunk around the rhinoceros' horn her favorite way, and floated her ears just gently above his back. The rhinoceros closed his eyes in relief and bliss, nibbling tenderly his beloved's lip.

After while they put the table and chairs back, and all the books and paintings and the bed. They lived the rest of their lives as a dancing elephant and a rich rhinoceros, with friends who came to dinner.

The Short Man and His Tall Wife

A man named Gerald was not tall. Gerald secretly admired tall people but, since he could do nothing about his size, he decided to live well as a short person. When he felt ready to marry, he looked for someone shorter than he—but fell in love with a woman a full head and a half too tall. Her name was Dinah.

Gerald could not help himself. He adored Dinah's leggy walk and the way she could stuff her hands into her pockets and still look willowy. "Just don't wear high heels," he told her.

"Sometimes?" she asked.

"Go ahead," Gerald said; but whenever Dinah

wore high heels, he tried not to look up into her face.

By the time they married, Dinah didn't really have many shoes with high heels, and with her wedding dress she wore white satin flats and dipped her head forward so her veil wouldn't make her too much taller than Gerald.

Dressing to go out to dinner to celebrate their first wedding anniversary, Dinah was helping Gerald dust off his blue suit coat. "Stand up straight, Sweetie," she said. "You're slouching."

"Standing up straight is tiring," Gerald said.

"I know," Dinah said, "but you look so handsome with your shoulders back and your head up tall."

Gerald stretched tall and inhaled mightily—then slumped again into the armpits of his coat. "Too hard," he said. "Let's go."

The dinner was lovely, and Dinah found she could still look up at Gerald by tipping her head sideways as well as dipping it forward.

Dinah and Gerald were married many years and had three babies who grew into children. Dinah developed back trouble and spent a lot of money on heating pads and chiropractors.

Gerald bent over with age because he had to sit at a desk all day as an accountant. He slouched his back and curled his shoulders until his chest was curved like a saucer and his back bowed out like a bowl.

"Stand tall," Dinah would chide gently. "You look so distinguished with your head up." But it made Gerald slouch more if she mentioned it, so all Dinah could do was bend her knees, to be shorter than Gerald.

The children grew up and moved away, leaving Gerald and Dinah to peer at each other from their recliners. One evening as Dinah struggled out of her chair to make the VCR record a Greta Garbo movie, Gerald noticed how warped and gnarled she was. His beautiful Dinah walked like a shrimp! He had not noticed it before. She was not lovely! She was deformed—a gnome, a monstrous parody of a little woman!

Gerald did not say anything to Dinah because he did not want to hurt her feelings. So he found a very tiny divorced secretary at his office, and they had an affair.

The Hare
and the
Tortoise

Once upon a time rivalry overheated, as rivalry can, between Tortoise and his friend Hare. So to decide, once and for all, who is faster—the Tortoise or the Hare—some townsfolk planned a race between them, and bet on who would win.

"Ho *ho*," said the grocer, "Tortoise'll show him what stamina is!"

"We're talking *speed* here," the mayor said. "Put my money on the rabbit."

"But does he run two minutes in the same direction?" asked the banker. "Hare's a flit."

"Hare may run fast," said the barber, "but you

have to follow the course to win a race. I'm betting on the shellback."

The townsfolk and racers laid out a course. Through the forest, around the meadow, and down a road back to the starting point the racetrack curled. Watchers were posted at intervals to keep the racers from taking a wrong turn. When the course was agreed upon and marked, the townspeople gathered at the starting point to place a bet and cheer a favorite.

At the starting gun's sound, both racers lunged onto the makeshift track. Tortoise pulled himself forward, straining so hard his leather stumps wobbled with effort. Hare shot down the track too fast to make dust. Only the watchers' glimpses of him zipping past the check points proved he was running the correct course.

Soon, though, Hare could keep neither his mind on the race nor his legs pumping smoothly. He wondered how the book he was reading at home would end. He remembered a bill he'd forgotten to pay. Then he noticed the forest trail was strewn with food wrappers, from boulder to tree trunk. He looked over his shoulder; Tortoise wasn't in sight.

I'll just tidy this, Hare decided. He stuffed the small trash into the bigger bags and boxes. A burst of speed got him to a garbage can and back just as Tortoise was coming over the rise into the forest. Hare waved to Tortoise, then took off running again.

Hare was running nicely, finding a good rhythm with three steps to a breath, when something plummeted to the trail ahead of him. Breathing hard, his fur damp from exertion, Hare slowed to see what it was. A baby bird, fallen from its nest, was chirping unconsolably. Nothing Hare could say soothed it.

"Then, we must," said Hare, "put you back in your nest."

Hare didn't tell the baby bird he'd never excelled at tree climbing. He clawed his way up the tree trunk, carrying the bird gently between his teeth. The bird's downy featherlets blew into Hare's nostrils, nearly smothering him, and if Hare didn't keep his head tipped back, saliva drenched the baby.

It was a trying five minutes, but Hare's joy at seeing the vulnerable bird safe in its nest assuaged his discomfort at speed-racing his dear slow friend. While clawing his way back down the tree, however, Hare fell the last ten feet to the ground and felt his delicate arch-bones become less perfectly articulated.

He limped a quarter mile down the trail before noticing he was trembling. Tree climbing had required muscles he didn't have, and those called upon to substitute were rioting with pain. So Hare, seeing Tortoise nowhere near, lay down to reduce his pain by relaxing deeply. Of course, he fell asleep.

Meanwhile, Tortoise clambered up the slopes of the trail and ambled down the inclines. Veering to neither right nor left, he wasted no energy chatting with observers, but saved his strength by merely smiling as he stroked past, one leg at a time dragging his boxy body forward.

Tortoise did notice how clean the trail was. And a pair of songbirds sounded especially joyful. But Tortoise's shell was rubbing his shoulders raw with every step. "Whose idea," he muttered, "was a speed race for a tortoise?" He tried to remember if he'd had the idea for this race first, or if it was the barber in town, a compulsive gambler. Tortoise was almost out of the woods and starting around the meadow now.

It startled Tortoise to see the rumpled pile of fur beside the path. Pulling himself by, foot over foot, he could see that Hare was sleeping deeply.

He's so bored, racing me, Tortoise thought, he can't even stay awake. I'm no challenge for a hare; this is not a real race. I *know* it was the barber. He continued his somber march toward the finish line crowded with townspeople.

Hare snored on, too tired to dream. But an image intruded upon his sleep. A bell was ringing, or an alarm, or a shrill whistle. Perhaps a birdcall in the woods, it woke Hare with a twitch. He looked around, completely lost. Seconds ticked by as he rubbed his eyes, trying to focus his mind through them. What was he doing by a path in the meadow?

The race! It came to him in one image. He was on his feet and running before he realized he had decided what to do. Around the edge of the meadow Hare ran, solidly in the inside lane. He made a clean turn onto the straightaway, the road into town, where the townsfolk were waiting to honor the victor.

There, nearing the finish line, was Tortoise. To Hare, just entering the final stretch, it looked as though Tortoise was touching the tape. Hare's heart pounded, and he put every ounce of strength into his dash down the road to town. He could hear his paws striking the hard-packed earth, thruppety-rupp, the very fastest his legs could go. He felt any moment they might tangle beneath his body and drop him to the ground. He begged them to keep going, as he fixed his eyes on the tape across the finish line.

Two steps before the finish line, Hare passed Tortoise. The tape snapped across his fuzzy chest in a triumphant "pfapp," and a grin widened Hare's face as his momentum carried him and the tape past the courthouse. Then he bounded back to Tortoise and pressed the finish tape onto his friend's shell with a moist furry hug.

Tortoise slowly extended his leather foot in congratulation. "Hare," he whispered into the tall velvet ear drooping to hear him, "some are simply faster than others."

But the townsfolk felt angry and cheated. Everyone knew how the story was supposed to end; some thought Hare had deliberately complicated the race.

"We'll have to run this again," the barber said, crumpling the bets in his fist.

"It's not *ever* legal to leave the track!" yelled a farmer at the mayor, who covered his ears and shouted, "All that matters is who breaks the tape!"

Someone shoved the banker, who had just lost

a considerable sum, and the banker kicked the wrong man in retaliation.

Turning away from the dust rising higher than the noise, Tortoise and Hare crossed the track and walked towards the meadow, to watch the sun set on the mountains. Hare was careful not to walk too fast, and Tortoise found an exquisitely soft peach-colored feather to give his dear friend Hare.

The Spider
Who Had
Potential

There was once a spider with enormous potential, destined to be one of the great web-spinners of all time. He knew it because he'd taken an aptitude test very young, and his parents said he was born with "the claws of a web-runner."

In school, the spider got the mystique down cold. He swaggered along walls and ran very lightly on his knuckles, "to save the claws." In the yearbook he was voted Spider With a Future, and he dated a lot.

Some of his spinning grades were low because certain teachers gave assignments that were too limiting, or too vague. But he could turn in fragments to other teachers and get A+'s on concept and originality. His work was too avant garde for many to understand, but he was so obviously talented that he got his glory early. He was serious and dedicated, a full-time difficult artist who would not work with deadlines.

Upon graduation, he needed to build a web to support himself. He found a patio with only light wind and a barbeque to draw flies, and began thinking of a spectacular web.

As he was deciding support strands might possibly be extended from a large fencepost to a nearby tree, two females from his school strolled by. One of them turned her front claws in toward each other and murmured to him, "I couldn't possibly spin anything as nice as yours will be; I'd be better off just sharing a web. I got such bad grades in design."

The spider with potential was slightly irritated by the interruption.

The female continued, "I always do the obvious—I'd probably just throw a strand from that fencepost to the tree and start spinning away. You'll do something so original for yours. I can hardly wait to see it." She edged closer.

"Where are you building?"

The potentially great spider tilted his head and squinted. "I like to absorb the ambience of a location before I start sketching."

The females climbed the frame of a plate glass window and began traditional Triangulars in the corners. They could look down on the fencepost and tree from their window.

The spider with potential couldn't concentrate with other spiders maybe watching him work. He curled into a ball to think about a special design, but by nightfall he'd spun only a lunch bag.

The next morning a friend stopped at the fencepost. "What's up?"

The spider with potential shrugged. "How're you doing?"

The friend shook his head. "Life's to learn from, right? Took me three hours to string a web in the backyard, and their dog ran through it in one second. Too low."

The spider nodded. It was incredibly stupid to build a low web in a yard with a dog. Had his friend *slept* through geography?

The friend clenched his claws. "This next one'll be low, too, but between those barbeque rungs so the dog'll have to trade his teeth for it."

He chuckled. "Guess you'll do something original and ambitious. Not me. I just want to catch a few juicy ones." He laughed sourly as he walked to the barbeque, where he started a standard Flat Rectangular between the barbeque legs.

The potentially great spider sat very still in the center of the fencepost to develop a visual concept, but every time he spun a little line to get the feel of the fiber, one of his classmates would smile and give him a thumbs-up. He couldn't concentrate.

He finally rolled the silk into a ball and absently tossed it back and forth among his claws. First left claw to first right claw, first left to second right, first left to third right, first left to fourth right; first right to first left, first right to second left . . . . He could see seventy-two permutations of the single tossing pattern. If he tossed the ball more than once to each claw, the permutations were infinite.

He spent the afternoon mastering the singles. He was amazingly smooth by nightfall.

When he looked up, it was too dark to see if the other spiders had finished their webs or caught any flies. He was ravenous. Everyone had complained about the stale flies at school, but even those sounded good right now.

He looked behind him toward the triangular webs in the window-corners, but the window was completely shadowed. He leaned over the edge of the post and closed his eyes to get used to the dark before he strained to see if his friend under the barbeque had anything—

He fell. It was a bad one. He couldn't breathe, couldn't move.

After a long time—he didn't know how long—the spider found a leg he could flex. Then he found another, and another, and another. He could straighten them, too. He thought he should turn onto his stomach and try to walk . . . .

Flipping over hurt, but walking brought a more painful discovery. As he crawled toward what he hoped was the fencepost, he tripped over something long and thin on the ground. One of his own legs! The horror of it made him retch.

The spider lay in the darkness, paralyzed by his loss. He was afraid to look at his leg or touch it. Or touch his body where the leg had been attached.

Then a larger fear filled him: he would die. Alone in the darkness, he would starve.

He wept.

At last the spider's fear hardened into determination, and he counted the legs he could move.

Six moved well, the seventh with care. He could even climb, slowly.

He left his eighth leg on the ground, and crept toward the fencepost. Cautiously, as evenly as possible, he climbed the post to the top. As he climbed, the blackness dissolved and he could see the wood beneath his claws.

He was tired and in shock, and he decided to save himself as simply as he could. He unwound the ball of silk he'd played with that afternoon, twisted it double, and made a short runway between the fencepost and the fence itself. He wove a circular web—the fewest lines, the shortest distances—finishing as the sun came up. He fell asleep at its edge, exhausted but hopeful.

He dreamed later that he was in a boat, surging, rocking, capsizing—and he awoke to find a large mosquito thrashing in his web. The mosquito whined and flailed, but the short simple strands of the circular web held firm. The spider, stiff and limping now, threw holding lines over the insect. Dodging the mosquito's piercing stylets, he killed and ate her.

The spider rested beside his web, waiting for nourishment to restore him. The sun glinted off the web, and he studied his project carefully.

The mosquito had torn a center strand, and one long span was attached to the fence at only its ends. A bee would have torn the web from the fence, and escaped.

The spider pulled himself to the long span, to weave broader end supports. He wove them tight and firm because he was still hungry and didn't want even a wasp to break his web.

As he was pulling a transverse cable as taut as he dared without breaking it, he suddenly realized that a taut web was *designed* to snap. An insect with any weight at all could break cables with no slack; in fact, the tight flat web gave it a platform from which to push off. A floppy web would wrap around a leg pushing off from it—entangle and exhaust a thrashing insect. The spider decided to try it.

He untied the base of the big transverse cable, and spun onto it three new cords which he coiled on the fencepost like springs. He carefully fastened the ends of the three cords to the post so they wouldn't tear loose, and laid the transverse cable back in its normal position. Then he replaced the ends of all the transverse cables with the triple-cord bases. Only the triple cords coiled almost invisibly around its edge made this web any more than a connected set of concentric circles as simple as a child's drawing. The spider backed into the crack between the post and fence, to wait.

He heard laughter, and someone yelling, "Mega-doilie!" But he was still hungry; so he stayed out of sight, crouching until his legs cramped, waiting for an insect to fly into his web, praying for the web to hold.

He saw a flash of metallic green, and the whole web lifted as though to fly. In a fumbling, thrashing scramble, an enormous blow fly tangled himself in the cords. What a treasure! The spider's heart pounded in his chest. He threw holding lines over the fly, balancing carefully on the swaying cables.

It was over in a moment. The stiff bristles that would have kept the blow fly just on the surface of a rigid web snagged him tighter in the flexible web. The spider was overwhelmed with happiness. The food would save his life, and his excitement was nearly uncontrollable at seeing his new idea work so well.

He looked around for someone to share his ecstasy. Down the post to the ground, and past the gate to the window, he discovered who'd been laughing and calling his web a doilie. But there was silence now.

His friend on the barbeque finally spoke. "Always said you'd do something original and ambitious. Just didn't expect that lace donut to work so well. How'd you do it?"

The spider showed his friends how to make the simple circular web and springs. Soon most of the newer webs were adapted from his design.

The spider refined his design and experimented with many others, always keeping his shapes pure and simple and their function foremost in his mind. He married his high school sweetheart, who now edited Web Weekly; he designed a community web to catch anything smaller than a hummingbird, for charity; and he spent a great deal of time teaching young spiders some things he'd learned in his life.

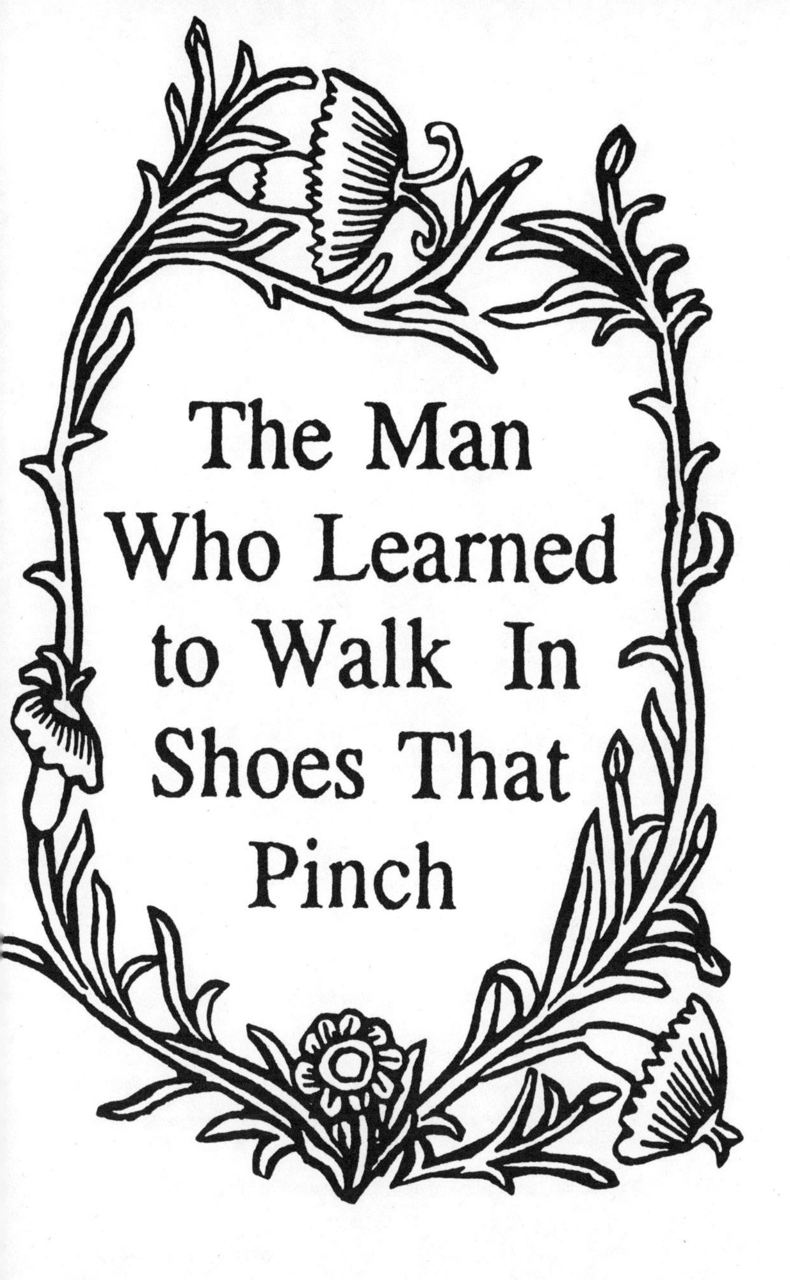

The Man
Who Learned
to Walk In
Shoes That
Pinch

ⓞnce upon a time a man bought a pair of
shoes that looked very handsome on his
feet. By the time he got home, however,
the shoes were pinching him terribly. It occurred
to him to return them to the store, but he remembered that his father'd always said, "Nobody likes
a complainer."

The man tried to stretch his new shoes with
shoe trees. He tried to soften the leather by bend-
ing it back and forth, back and forth. He decided
to wear thinner socks with these shoes. He laced
them looser.

The shoes were extremely well made, and the

man felt dashing in them. But they pinched his feet as painfully as ever.

The man discovered that if he pulled his toes back into a clump the shoes didn't hurt quite so much. He found, though, that the dull pain made him stoop a little and place his feet more carefully when he walked.

When he first put his shoes on in the morning, they hurt him very much, but by the time he got to work, his feet were numb and he didn't feel them any more. He was learning to walk faster with his toes curled. And by swinging his arms a bit harder, he could walk quite well bent forward. But it did interfere with his breathing.

The man had responsibilities and eventually forgot about his shoes. He put them on each morning, curled his toes, bent over, pumped his arms, breathed tiny puffs of air, and carried on with his work.

A year later his handsome shoes were no longer new. The soles were worn thin, the heels were run over, and the stitching was loose in two places. The man returned to the store to buy new shoes.

"What size do you take?" asked the salesman.

"I don't know," said the man.

The salesman picked up the old shoes and

looked inside. "12-B," he said. And he brought the man five pairs of stylish new shoes to choose from.

The man selected a smart-looking pair of cordovan wing-tips that cost a great deal of money. He curled his toes, bent over, pumped his arms, and sucked in tiny puffs of air as he walked to the cash register to pay for his handsome new shoes.

The wing-tips were heavier than his other shoes, so he had to bend over a little farther and pump his arms a little harder, to walk with much speed. He could breathe in only little squirts of air this way, his back was developing a great hump from being bent all day, and the pain was making him clench and grind his teeth. The only advantage was that with his face so close to the ground he often found money other people had lost. He once discovered a twenty-dollar bill floating in a gutter.

During that year the man had to have all his teeth extracted and false teeth fitted. But he found a total of $67.84, two different fourteen carat gold earrings, and a mother-of-pearl key ring.

It took the man years to wear out his wing-tip shoes because it was so uncomfortable to walk now, that he rode everywhere he possibly could. His legs atrophied a little, and his feet shrank a bit; his eyes grew weaker because he looked mostly at the ground, which was never more than a few feet from his face. He huffed and puffed, inhaled and exhaled, but his lungs began filling with fluid because he never straightened his torso anymore.

The longer he stayed bent, the harder it was for his heart to pump. The harder it was for his heart to pump, the more fluid seeped into his poor squashed lungs.

At last the wing-tips wore out, and the man took a taxi to the shoe store to buy some brand new shoes. He was very excited.

The salesman noted, in the wing-tips, that the man was a 12-B, so he brought his finest new 12-B's for the little bent man to see. The man peered at the shiny new shoes and stroked the smooth leather with his fingertips. He hefted the shoes for weight and noticed the crepe soles on the casual ones.

He was enjoying the new-shoe smell of a lovely caramel-colored loafer when, in his excitement, a drop of saliva caught in his bent-over windpipe. The man coughed and hacked, choked and gasped. In his paroxysms, the fluid in his lungs frothed and burbled and got in the way. His false teeth slipped from his gums, compounding his problems. The man turned blue, bulged his eyes, and grabbed the salesman, who didn't know what to do except slap him on the back.

That was exactly the wrong thing to do. The man snapped in two and died on the spot, before they could even call an ambulance.

The morticians sewed the man back together for his funeral. They combed his hair and dressed him in his favorite double-breasted pinstripe suit with coordinated French-cuffed shirt and red silk tie. But when they put his shoes on him, he bent over too far to fit in his coffin unless they turned him sideways.

The Hamster and the House Mouse

One midnight a hamster was running in his exercise wheel when a house mouse pressed his fuzzy gray face between the wires of the cage.

"Where are you going?" sneered the mouse.

The hamster slowed to a gentle roll to decide how to handle the mouse's sarcasm. "I'm going to be healthy."

The mouse rolled onto his back and waved his paws in the air, laughing until he gasped.

The hamster sped up and concentrated on breathing evenly, letting the mouse become a blur on the floor.

"Come outside!" the mouse said. "I'll show you how to open this cage."

"Oh, I can open it," the hamster said. "This is my home."

"You call a *cage* your *home*?" the mouse shrieked.

The hamster didn't feel like defending his home to a stranger. But he said, "My family is terrific. The food is fresh, and—"

"Your food is not what they eat," countered the mouse. "You should see what they eat! They give you dry seeds, while they eat steak!"

"But I—" the hamster began.

"You're being humiliated!" Indignation filled the mouse.

"No," the hamster said. "They offer me everything they have. If I love something, I wolf it and stuff some in my pouches so they'll give me more. If a food is just okay, I nibble it. If something's really awful and I don't want to be bothered with it again, I turn around and refuse to look at it. Humans are pretty sharp; they catch on."

"You're a captive, a victim, a dupe!" the mouse yelled.

"How do you know?" asked the hamster.

The mouse snorted derisively.

"This is a delightful family," the hamster said. "We play every day; they keep this . . . cage in top shape . . . ."

"You're being patronized!" The mouse spat the words. "You are not free!"

"I am free," the hamster said. "I can leave any time and run behind the refrigerator. But they would chase me; they wouldn't trust me any more. We have a relationship you perhaps don't understand."

The mouse looked desperate.

"Okay," the hamster said. "I have an open hour. You want to go be free together?"

The mouse nearly wept with gratitude as the hamster squeezed past his cage door.

"Where do you want to go first?" the hamster asked.

"The kitchen! Let me teach you something about freedom!"

They scurried along baseboards and darted across doorways in case owls were perching on the chandeliers.

The mouse scuttled across the kitchen floor ahead of the hamster and stopped in front of a wastebasket. He hauled himself up the basket, gasping, "Follow me!"

"That's garbage!" said the hamster. "We throw that away!"

"They throw it away," the mouse grunted, "because the pieces are too small. But it's perfectly good stuff. Much better than the swill they feed you."

"We'll see," the hamster said. He scrambled up the wastebasket after the house mouse and looked at the array of boxes, bottles, cartons, and discarded food. He was about to fling himself off the edge of the basket to play in the maze of tunnels among the boxes when the mouse spoke.

"Look for bones and fancy wrappers; they mean good stuff. Like this." The mouse pulled out a croissant box with a fleur de lis and the words LA PATISSERIE on top. "Taste these," the mouse insisted.

The hamster nibbled flakes of croissant in the lovely box. The croissant coated his teeth with grease, but he said, "Very nice."

The mouse nodded triumphantly and tossed the box back into the trash. He dived forward and burrowed noisily. In a moment he surfaced, dragging a large t-bone. "They didn't offer you this," the mouse challenged. "Porterhouse. I read the wrapper."

"I don't eat much red meat," the hamster said.

"Let's be honest; you don't eat any."

The hamster rose into his attack posture and bared his teeth.

"Cut that out," the mouse said. "Gnaw this."

The hamster chewed a bit of gristle off the end of the bone, experimented with the marrow, and found some strands of tenderloin stuck to the bone. "Thanks," he said, though he could scrape cold fat from the roof of his mouth with his tongue.

Next, the house mouse presented a piece of chocolate cake, with most of its frosting intact. "Dessert!" he crowed. "Start on that side; I'll meet you in the middle." He dug in enthusiastically.

The hamster started nibbling, but the frosting stuck his fingers together, and the cake made his teeth feel rough when he rubbed his tongue across them. His stomach felt dangerously queasy, and his head ached. He leaned back on his haunches. "Anything to drink here?"

The mouse nodded and dived into the trash. He resurfaced with a can of Diet Pepsi. "Tip it sideways and let the Pepsi pool here where you can get your mouth in." He dived back into the trash for another can. "I'll join you."

"Here's a carrot," the hamster said, reaching for

a limp orange corpse of a vegetable.

"Ugh!" The mouse shuddered.

"It isn't fresh," the hamster apologized. "They give me the ends of fresh ones . . . ." He realized, too late, how second-rate that sounded. "I like just a little at a time; the ends are the perfect size." It sounded lame.

"Weeds," the mouse muttered, burying the carrot in the trash. He dove again and returned with a salami sandwich, beer bottle, and wet wine cork. "They're warm," he said, "but try these."

"No, thanks," the hamster said. "I'm fine."

"You're a prude!" the mouse yelled. "Loosen up. Get free! *Live!*" He grabbed the wine cork and chewed off most of the end. "You don't know what you're missing," he crooned.

"You can finish the cork," the hamster said. "I'll have a little of the sandwich."

The mayonnaise coated the hamster's tongue, and the salami gave him heartburn. He stood up to rub his stomach. He wanted to curl into a ball and sleep until he felt better. He was dying of thirst, but he wanted plain water. "Can we get up on the sink?" he asked the mouse.

"Nothing up there. Everything's in the cupboards or trash. You want to be careful of eating stuff in the cupboards, though; if they see teethmarks, they'll put out traps."

Traps! the hamster thought. Every day my family carries me in someone's pocket, rocks me to sleep, hand-feeds me apples and carrots, and gives me back rubs. And this mouse feels free dodging traps!

But his thoughts were interrupted by a gasping and scrambling from the mouse. "Give me a paw!" the mouse wheezed. "Help me up!"

The hamster hopped off the croissant box and rolled the house mouse onto his feet. The exertion made the hamster feel worse; he knew he'd throw up. "I'm going home," he said.

"Wait," the mouse said. "You haven't seen the crackers."

"I feel sick," the hamster said. "I'll be honest with you: If they eat this stuff and give me seeds and fruit, they love me more than I thought." He climbed carefully down the trash basket, then turned back to the mouse. "Thanks for the invitation. I do value options."

The hamster threw up on the floor and crawled back to his cage. His stomach was so tender he couldn't squeeze into his cage; he stretched out on top of it and fell asleep.

In the morning he was awakened by a shriek from the kitchen. "A dead mouse in the wastebasket!" The mother of his family carried the wastebasket past his cage and out the door.

There on top of the croissant box lay the house mouse—his gray fur matted, his paws stiffened above his bloated stomach, his mouth open forever now, the long yellow teeth curved to bite eternally.

As the house mouse passed on his bier, the hamster stood and bowed his head. Then he wriggled back into his cage and climbed into his exercise wheel.

The Woman Who Couldn't Let Go

There was once a woman who had trouble getting rid of anything she'd ever liked.

As a teenager, when she outgrew clothes, she put them in suitcases and saved them in the attic. In her twenties, she rescued toasters, irons, vacuum cleaners, lamps, and phonographs that broke after years of faithful service. She placed them loyally on shelves in the garage.

Of course, she couldn't marry because she'd have to leave her parents and the home of her childhood. Eventually, however, her parents died and left her alone in the house she'd grown up in. She packed their things in tissue paper, in trunks, and converted their bedroom into a storage room.

Most magazines and nearly all books had to be stored—and newspapers of important days—until her father's study gradually filled with boxes so heavy that silverfish caught in the bottom boxes were trapped, airless, to dry into mummies.

She bought a new car every ten or fifteen years, but never sold an old one. She couldn't forget the lovely places she'd driven in the cars. So she stored each one on blocks in the garage until she had to start putting them in the tool shed, the potting shed, and, finally, the patio.

Of course, she saved the furniture, art work, jewelry, and dishes of her parents and grandparents. She also saved their tools and utensils, cosmetics and spices, razors and curling irons, TV trays and shower shoes. She saved Wheaties boxes and Mickey Mouse spoons, pretty bottles and plastic flowers, unusual bottlecaps and colorful stamps, matchbook covers and garden sprinklers. She saved everything she'd ever liked.

Any pet she bought as a puppy, kitten, or baby bird or fish lived out its last blind, toothless, balding, tumorous, cranky days with her because the woman could not bear to have any pet put to sleep.

Eventually, she grew old and feeble herself. It became more and more difficult for her to get around, as the pathways between the boxes and trunks narrowed, while her own joints stiffened and her eyes dimmed. Her last dog, a blind, deaf, arthritic St. Bernard with a wheezing condition, was an additional hazard because he could neither see nor hear that he needed to get out of the way, nor could he see or hear where to go.

At last one day the old woman was found dead, sprawled across the St. Bernard, but reaching in the direction of the telephone. Experts surmised that she had suffered a heart attack but been prevented from summoning help by the enormity and immobility of the dog. Anyway, the telephone was wedged between a carton of her favorite cheese labels and a trunk of antique dolls; she could never have wrenched the receiver free in her weakened state.

Her will was read with great curiosity because she had no descendants. It revealed that the woman had bequeathed all her worldly possessions to the city zoo, site of cherished childhood memories.

The zoo director was the first to see the old woman's house. He was horrified, then furious.

It was a trick, he raged—a hoax wasting the time of already overworked zoo personnel.

But his assistant, a young slim man with bright brown eyes, peeked in some of the boxes and squeezed himself down the passageways leading to all the overstuffed rooms. He asked to be in charge of the case. The director agreed.

The young assistant was an avid collector of antiques and nostalgia pieces. He recognized the old woman's home as a warehouse of treasure—and a fine gift to the zoo. He catalogued the materials and marketed them shrewdly, amassing a gift of two and a half million tax-free dollars from the old woman to her fondly remembered zoo.

The assistant, who soon became director of the zoo, used the money to build an animal nursery and a huge paddock full of furry animals to be petted and squeezed by children. The nursery and paddock were named after the old woman in an impressive ceremony attended by the mayor, zoo board members, and many school children. The woman's profile, in bronze, was embedded like a big cheerful penny in one wall of the paddock, and wonderful stories were printed in all the newspapers about the fine old woman who left her immense fortune to the children and furry animals of her city.

The Fly

An enormous black fuzzy fly lived rather quietly in a house overlooking the ocean. It wasn't his house; that is, he didn't maintain it. He simply lived in it.

Every day the woman who owned the house found the fly and tried to kill him. She'd follow him with a fly swatter or folded newspaper, Dipteracide her goal. But the fly's technique was always the same: He'd let the woman get quite close and take one mighty swing, causing air turbulence that allowed him to dive to the floor with an injured "Bzzzzrrrt" and roll under a piano or behind a television or bookcase—

something immovable.

He then held his breath in absolute silence while the woman moved chairs and piano benches, trumpet cases and wood baskets, hoping to find him dead or stunned on the floor so she could finish him off. Eventually, the woman would lose interest and go away. The fly could then tiptoe out of hiding and enjoy the rest of his day in peace, as long as he didn't make noise or fly into a room where the woman was. It was a careful life.

Once, when the woman had actually stunned him and left him for dead in a waste basket, he came to and didn't know where he was. The experience sobered him, leaving him far more spiritual and aware of life's evanescence.

Other flies, however, scorned his technique. "You hurt our image," they complained. "Humans have no respect for us; standing up to them allows us at least a final dignity. You're so big that your stand would have impact. We're so small no one notices."

"How do you think I got so big?" asked the fly. But no one listened.

"My philosophy—" he began. But they shouted him down.

He saw, later that afternoon, a small smooth fly

watching the woman out of the tops of his eyes as she closed in on him against a pair of French doors. At the last second, the small fly turned to the woman and made an obscene gesture, which left its defiant imprint in his blood against the glass.

The other flies were moved. When the woman Windexed the fly's body from the glass, the other flies vowed to speck the entire glass door, from hinge to handle, in his memory.

The large fly, uncomfortable with their decision, decided to move out of the house. He found a pet shop with plenty of company and food, where the owners didn't chase him if he didn't buzz. In fact, he was growing large enough to look like a pet. His low profile during the day allowed him a little time to buzz before bed after the shop closed.

A week after he moved to the pet shop, he heard from a wasp that the small flies' insurrection over the French door incident had grown ugly. Besides specking both French doors, the flies had buzzed loudly at night near every lamp in the house, and incited the normally reticent fruit flies to dash into the eyes of the woman.

"They backed her to the wall," the wasp said.

"What happened?" asked the fly.

"She bought an insect fogger," the wasp said, his eyes still bright with terror. "Everybody's gone—spiders, roaches, anyone with wings."

"What did they expect?" the fly asked. Neither he nor the wasp could answer.

The fly felt old without the other flies. He ate a lot, and buzzed absently.

But upon reflection, he realized it wasn't the other flies he missed, but someone he'd never known. He wanted to meet someone who really talked and actually listened—someone with ideas and curiosity, who didn't doubt a plan simply because it had never been tried. Someone who didn't live just for a swarm.

The fly observed the other animals in the pet shop. He interviewed them, to figure out what made them pets instead of pests. It was a contemplative life. He grew larger and stronger, eating the Hi-Proteen Puppy Chow Early Growth Formula because that bin was always uncovered.

One day, buzzing the parakeet mirrors, the fly nearly went into cardiac arrest from fear. He was so big that even from a foot away he could see only his head and neck in a single mirror.

"I'm enormous," he gasped. "They'll see me and swat. I won't live to see tomorrow."

He hid behind the hamster cages until dark. But he thought of a plan.

He got two parrots to help him drag the shop's smallest bird cage into the display window. Then he had a monkey make a sign for him:

SEE THE WORLD'S LARGEST FLY!
HE FLIES! HE BUZZES! HE DANCES!

The fly didn't know if he was the very largest, but he considered hype necessary in show business. And he really intended to practice his dancing.

He climbed into the cage and waited for the shopkeeper to arrive in the morning. It was a risk. She could be disgusted and swat him on the spot. But he'd still have a chance to dash between the bars and escape. It was worth the risk. And it excited him.

When the shopkeeper arrived, the fly looked her in the eyes and tilted his head, laying his bristles flat, like fur.

The shopkeeper stood very still, reading the sign, watching the fly.

As dramatically and smoothly as he could, the fly lifted his wings and twirled across the floor of the cage, one spin after another, perfectly balanced, in a straight line. At the opposite side, he stopped, turned a cartwheel, and bowed. Holding the bow, he held his breath and watched the pet shop owner out of his eye-tops.

The owner was smiling. She lifted both hands to the cage . . . .

The fly tensed . . . .

The owner applauded. "You have charisma."

The shopkeeper gave the fly a bigger cage with a resined floor, a professionally painted sign, and his own dish of Hi Proteen Puppy Chow. She even put vitamin drops in his water and an assortment of dance videos in the VCR so the fly could learn new routines on days when there weren't many customers to entertain.

The fly lived a long and happy life, enormously pleased that the shop owner gave him credit right out loud for the sudden 22 1/2% increase in the shop's walk-in traffic.

The
Toad
Who Knew
It All

There was once a toad who went to the city and learned all about the world. While he was there he learned *everything*.

It was so important that he wrote it all into a large book which he carried with him wherever he went. The toad carried his book pressed against his heart so he would never forget what he had learned and would always know precisely what to do.

One day the toad was crossing a river on a fallen log. With his enormous book pressed against his heart, he could not see where he was walking, and he tripped over a knot in the log. The toad made one anguished squeak as he slid off the log and into the river.

The current was running swiftly, and the toad needed both hands to save himself by grabbing the edge of the bank. But he dared not let go of his book of everything.

The toad with his book tumbled down the river, head over binding. At last the book became water-logged and sank; and the toad, clutching it against his heart, drowned.

The
Silver
Dollar

There were once fraternal twins named Wheeler and Albert. For their twelfth birthday they each received, among other gifts, a shiny new silver dollar fresh from the mint.

"Fantastic!" Albert said. That afternoon he skateboarded to a Speedimart, bought a dollar's worth of candy, and ate it on the way home.

Wheeler put his silver dollar in the secret pocket of his wallet while he decided how to use it. His Aunt Cynthia asked what he got for his birthday, and when he showed her the silver dollar, she asked what he was going to buy.

"Well," Wheeler said, "I can't buy much with a dollar, so I may save it."

"Smart boy!" Aunt Cynthia said. "Have a cookie!"

Wheeler enjoyed it so much that she gave him two more.

That afternoon Wheeler bicycled to Wholesome Farms Market to buy tofu and grapefruit for his mother. On the way he stopped at Le Scoop for his Free Birthday Scoop and to see if the disarmingly gorgeous ice cream-scooper was working that day. She wasn't. Just the owner was, but he turned out to be her father, Arnold Simms. Mr. Simms asked Wheeler what he got for his birthday. Wheeler told him and held up the silver dollar.

"That's a double," Simms said.

"Could be," Wheeler answered, "but I'm saving it toward something big. Your ice cream is great, but I don't want to spend a silver dollar."

"Certainly," Simms said. Then, making sure no one else was in the store, "We'll make this birthday cone a double, for a wise and thrifty young man."

Wheeler thanked Mr. Simms very much, and selected Almond Fudge and Praline Cheesecake on a sugar cone. He ate it in the store, chatting with

Simms about the amount of capital required to buy a successful franchise.

The next morning, Wheeler's father wanted to borrow a couple of dollars, fast, for lunch because he'd forgotten to cash a check. Wheeler was adamant. No one could borrow his silver dollar, and his other money was in his passbook account. So the father grabbed a couple of dollars from Albert and rushed out the door, promising to pay him back right after work.

But a man who forgets to cash a check for his own food will not remember to cash a check for a small debt. So, after several weeks of reminders and promises magneted to the refrigerator, the two dollars disappeared forever into the great family vault of forgotten favors and forgiven sins.

That summer, Mr. Simms offered Wheeler a job at Le Scoop and, when the store wasn't busy, the two of them discussed investments and coin collecting. Simms advised Wheeler to keep his silver dollar where it wouldn't get scratched, and they checked the till daily for collectible coins. They never found much. Wheeler sold the few good coins he found in the till, but he put his silver dollar, in a special coin envelope, in a safe deposit box a local bank was giving as a free promotional offer to children who started a college account. Wheeler used his Le Scoop earnings to open the account.

The next year, the price of silver soared, and many silver dollars like Wheeler's were pulled out of circulation and melted into belt buckles and Indian rings. But Wheeler kept his in the safe deposit box.

In his first year in high school Wheeler wrote a short messy term paper on the stock market and, as part of his research, interviewed a stock broker named George Hemmling. Hemmling thought that, by befriending Wheeler, he could become Wheeler's parents' stock broker.

Because Wheeler's college account had grown to over two thousand dollars, Hemmling could get Wheeler into a money market account with Hemmling's brokerage firm Deeter Pinkus. At Deeter Pinkus Wheeler could double the interest rate he'd been getting on his old passbook account, buy stock, and talk to Hemmling about his investment ideas. But Wheeler left the two hundred dollar minimum in his bank account, to keep the safe deposit box for his silver dollar. Hemmling helped Wheeler buy a very safe utility stock and some zero coupon treasury bills for his college fund.

Hemmling told a newspaper reporter friend about Wheeler, and the reporter wrote a story on Wheeler as the youngest investor in town. Wheeler's photo showed him holding his silver dollar in one hand and his stock certificates in the other.

The editor of the school paper saw the article and asked Wheeler if he'd like to write a Dear Wheeler financial column in the school paper. Wheeler loved it. He researched his answers carefully, in books and with Deeter Pinkus experts and Mr. Simms.

For his job that summer, Wheeler worked at Deeter Pinkus, as a delivery boy and doing a promotional campaign for parents to start children's college funds with Deeter Pinkus. Wheeler's photo, holding his now-famous silver dollar and his stocks and treasury bills, were in magazines and newspapers all over the country. Deeter Pinkus had their top portfolio management team advise Wheeler so his earnings grew exceptionally well.

Wheeler traveled around the country for Deeter

Pinkus, appearing on talk shows with the D-P vice-president who now personally handled Wheeler's account. Wheeler's poise and self-confidence grew with his reputation, and he was asked to write his Dear Wheeler column for the local newspaper. He had to hire a talent agent to negotiate his commercials and speaking engagements.

The bank asked Wheeler if they could display his silver dollar beside other famous coins in a glass vault for their centennial celebration. Wheeler's agent said no, but agreed when the bank gave Wheeler free checking, travelers' checks, and safe deposit box for life.

During Wheeler's senior year in high school, the stock market fell precipitously, and Wheeler lost several thousand dollars on his stocks before his adviser could sell his steel and petroleum holdings. The lesson sobered Wheeler, and he became an even more sensitive student of the economy and human psychology.

That same year, though, gold and silver prices rose again, and Wheeler's silver dollar was worth $11.75 just in silver content. But, of course, it was worth a million in his commercials and personal appearances. He didn't even consider selling it.

Selective universities around the nation vied for Wheeler and he got a nice scholarship, though he didn't actually need it, to attend his first choice. He majored in economics and syndicated his Dear Wheeler column in 276 newspapers across the country. Of course, now his advice was for young adults and their parents.

Wheeler had so much money invested with Deeter Pinkus that he qualified for their Super Gold Premium Account, which gave him a gold-plated credit card good all over the world, a million dollar line of credit, detailed weekly statements of his transactions, a private line to his broker, no broker fees, and a Preferred Client interest rate on his money market account.

Wheeler finished his Ph.D. at his first-choice graduate school, and his dissertation explaining how to protect the world economy from interlinked national economic crises was published and became a best-seller.

Wheeler married an Italian princess he'd met in graduate school, and they were able to buy an estate in upstate New York by paying cash for its back taxes. By modernizing its plumbing, heating, and electrical systems, they made it into an extremely comfortable, and even economical, house.

From the wing Wheeler converted into his office, he wrote a newsletter that influenced the stock market so heavily that when Wheeler vacationed twice a year, the DOW fell just from uncertainty. Wheeler sat on the boards of Deeter Pinkus and all its rivals until he had to divest himself of those positions in order to become a Presidential economic adviser.

Wheeler worked very effectively, and even when he vacationed he brought home more money than he spent. Airlines and cruise ships insisted on transporting him as their guest, and foreign governments took him in limos to banquets in his honor and presidential palaces to stay. He was showered with gifts.

When Wheeler turned forty, the hopelessly snarled economy was the country's biggest problem, and the only economist everyone knew and trusted was Wheeler. Wheeler was elected President in a landslide, and he saved not just the U.S., but the world, economy in his two terms.

As he sat in the Oval Office, silver-sideburned

and internationally beloved, his silver dollar was worth $2,856.00 because there were only fourteen silver dollars left from that year. The others had been melted into silver bullion, belt buckles, and Indian rings.

But Wheeler discovered his silver dollar's actual value when he flew in the Presidential jet to visit his twin brother Albert that winter.

Albert and his wife Naomi were paying triple the going rate to heat their house because their old inefficient furnace wasted fuel, but they couldn't afford to replace it. Buying so much fuel for the wasteful heater, they ran out of money and had to borrow money to pay for fuel, adding interest payments to the cost of the fuel. They couldn't make the payments on time, so a fine was added. Because their credit rating was so bad, they couldn't borrow the money to pay for a whole year's supply of fuel to be delivered all at once. They were forced to pay monthly delivery fees when the truck brought each month's supply, instead of one delivery fee for a year's supply.

Actually, Albert, Naomi, and their six children couldn't replace the bad furnace because they were renting the house; they'd never been able to scrape together a down payment. They owned their car, but it burned oil besides gas because it needed an expensive ring job.

Albert and Naomi owed interest and extra fees on all their credit cards, and had to pay for their checking account, travelers checks, safe deposit box, and money orders. Fortunately, they didn't want to invest, because they had so little money no brokers wanted them for clients.

Wheeler sat by their furnace a long time, warming his hands, trying to think of something to do for Albert, Naomi, and the children without hurting their feelings. Finally, he whispered instructions to an assistant, who returned in a few hours with six large gift-wrapped packages and a box of Presidential stationery. With his Presidential pen, Wheeler wrote six letters and slipped one into each package.

Wheeler gave one present to each of Albert and Naomi's children. Each child's gift contained an unabridged dictionary, computer, paper and pens, a set of school clothes, a letter from Uncle Wheeler inviting them to visit him *often* and talk about life—and a silver dollar fresh from the mint.

The Rug Weaver and the Collector

There was once a red-haired city man who collected Indian rugs. He hung them on his walls, spread them on his floor, and used a soft one as a bedspread. He pored over the rugs and read books about their symbolism until he could find clouds, lightning, waterbugs, mountains, and spirit lines in his rugs.

But the images in the rugs were drawn from the weavers' lives, and the collector feared that he could not understand a rug until he understood the weaver's life. Surely, he decided, weavers saw mountains precisely at dawn. Certainly they drank purer water and saw wilder beasts than a city man could possibly experience on two-week guided tours of the wilderness. The collector became obsessed with discovering the rugs' truths in the weavers' lives.

At his favorite Indian reservation the next summer, the collector spoke alone to the very best weaver. "Come home with me," he told her. "Show me where you find the truths you weave into your rugs."

The Indian smiled at him. "They are wherever I look."

The collector persisted. "You pull your designs from your life. I want to *see* the truths you put in your rugs."

The Indian squinted at him. "My designs are in my rugs; my truths are in my rugs. My life is the life I live so I can weave. You'll be happier hanging the *rugs* on the wall—not *me*."

But the collector insisted, offering the weaver more and more money until she finally could not resist. "All right," she said, "a weaver *is* more and less than a rug."

"Fine!" the collector said. "You will live with me in the city and show me how you pull your designs from life."

The Indian lovingly packed her loom, fleece, beaters, heddle rods, cards, spindle, pouches of dried roots, mortar and pestle—and took them and her clothes to the city with the collector. It was exciting at first. The collector hung on the weaver's every word; she felt important. The weaver was fascinated by the collector's city life and began weaving sky scrapers and automobiles into her rugs.

The collector, however, discovered things he didn't like about the weaver: her fingers were always a different color. Her loom was enormous and made lint, and her room was so full of yarns and threads that she stacked baskets of fleece in the hallway. The weaver spent her nights on the balcony watching city lights, and her dawns in the park, stalking birds. She wore soft clothes that were easy to weave in but didn't look nice in the city.

"Couldn't you dress up for dinner, read these books, lunch at this restaurant, go to bed earlier, come to these parties, and grow your fingernails out?" asked the collector.

"No," said the weaver. "That's a collector. I'm a weaver." She looked at the collector a long time before she smiled.

The collector was patient a few more days until the weaver stayed up past three one morning watching city lights—then came inside and began weaving them into her rug.

The noise made the collector so furious that he stormed into the weaver's room, cut her rug off the loom, rolled her up in it, and set her out for the trash collectors, who were coming by at nine. He dumped all her equipment next to her on the sidewalk.

The weaver rolled downhill to free herself from the rug, telephoned a cousin who had a pickup truck, and returned to the reservation. She finished the rug the collector had cut from the loom, though it had to be short with its warp threads cut.

Some years later, in his favorite uptown gallery, the collector recognized the short rug hanging on a wall, a spotlight illuminating its moonlit skyscrapers, speed-blurred car lights, jeweled ladies, and long-legged gentlemen. The moonlight looked so real, and the buildings so tall, the collector felt dizzy.

He stepped back, to see if the rug's composition had been damaged by being shortened so abruptly. No, the moon was just easier for the buildings to reach. The collector put on his glasses, to see if the price listed on the little white card beside the rug had been lowered for its shortness. No, the price was higher than he'd imagined.

But, there! Woven into the corner of the rug was a tiny red-haired man facing out into the gallery, his arms reaching for something, his fingers groping.

The collector adjusted his glasses and peered at the questing man, whose tiny nose, ears, and fingers had been woven with amazing skill. His little suit had buttons; his tie had stripes. But there, where his eyes should have been, were two small empty holes.

The
Potter

A potter named Mirabel considered herself an Artist. Her potter's wheel, the instrument of her muse, connected directly to that stream of inspiration which encircles the earth and to which only a few fortunate people ever attach. Mirabel threw pots for six hours every day and got headaches if she had to do anything else for her life's work.

To earn food and shelter, however, Mirabel needed to *sell* her pots—in galleries and boutiques. Unfortunately, other people did not see Mirabel's pots as works of Art. Most saw her Experimental Forms as large sturdy flower vases and dishwasher-safe salad bowls.

Mirabel was horrified to see her Pure Sculptural Shapes used as household objects. Whenever a gallery owner displayed her pots holding silk flowers, to give customers ideas, Mirabel indignantly removed her work from the gallery.

"These are *sculptures*," she'd say, "with texture, line, and color. People can't stick salad and flowers in Art!"

But when her landlord put a FOR RENT sign on the front door of her apartment, it occurred to Mirabel that if she couldn't sell her pots as *something*, she'd have to go back to work at the dry cleaners.

So she closed her eyes and spun her potter's wheel to draw inspiration from the stream encircling the earth. Eagerly, she pedaled, squeezing the clay lump on her wheel. Clay swelled upward between her thumbs and fingers, changing shape faster than clouds boiling in wind—and Mirabel realized that her art was meant to bring other people joy in its use, as it brought her joy in its creation. Clay is earth; Mirabel was a shaper of earth. She must not keep the earth from its people. Inspiration from the encircling stream told Mirabel exactly what to do, and Mirabel did it:

Every day, alone with her muse, Mirabel connected to the stream encircling the earth and created works of Art. She lived a pure uncompromised life, discovering each day what her creativity could bring forth. She did, however, finish and smooth the insides of the sculptures, and make sure they were deep enough to hold long stems. She did also notice which glazes sold fastest at what galleries, and she developed microwave-safe sculptures.

Once a month, when she fired her creations in her kiln, she visualized them annealing into immortal treasures for the pantheon of Artists. Then, removing the treasures from the kiln, Mirabel nestled her works of Art in tissue paper and styrofoam, in boxes she delivered to art galleries, museum shops, and boutiques. She left her sculptures at the galleries and shops—she, one of the luckiest, happiest people in the world: an Artist.

The gallery and shop owners unwrapped the salad bowls and cookie jars, selecting salad sets and kitchen towels to compliment their glazes. They chose silk flowers for the vases and trivets for the microwave-safe casserole dishes. The owners considered themselves the most fortunate entrepreneurs in the world to handle nearly exclusive sales of these hand-thrown, exquisitely-crafted household objects decorators loved and customers adored.

The
Runt

There was once a litter of pigs with an unusually small runt. Further, the runt had short upright ears and a long furry tail that didn't curl well. The other piglets taunted him, through slimy snouts.

First, the runt tried being witty. But the other piglets weren't amused. Next, the runt tried athleticism. He could climb to the top of the sty and jump off onto a manure pile, when the other piglets could barely waddle to the top of the pile. But flashy climbing and jumping irritated the piglets. They sat on him.

One noon, the runt noticed he'd spent the whole

morning climbing the sty and jumping off—while the other piglets cozied in the mud wallow. He realized he was living his life alone. "Is this good?" he asked himself. "Am I missing something important?"

He smoothed his tail across the least-splintered part of the pigsty roof, and curled onto it, to think. His mind wandered.

Above him spread the branches of an enormous oak tree, with hollows in the biggest limbs and the trunk. As the runt noticed the tree bark swelling around the hollows, upholstering their openings, and the branches swarming from the trunk to the sunlight so their leaves could get their share, he was filled with an ecstasy so powerful it frightened him. Staring into the tree gave him personal certainty which, as a runt, he had never known.

The tree arched as broad as the sky, above the runt, drawing him toward it. He knew this tree without knowing how he knew. The hairs on his ears stood up. Is this how obsessions begin, he worried. Or is this insight?

As the runt was trying to figure out how to get up into the tree, a small furred animal with a magnificent floating tail scurried down the branch above the pigsty, and disappeared into a hollow.

The bark crackled beneath the creature's claws. The creature popped out of the hollow, ran up the branch to the trunk of the tree, then down the trunk to the ground.

"So that's it!" the runt said.

Strengthened by a force he felt no need to explain, he leaped off the sty onto the manure pile, ran across the mud to the fence—and stopped. Piglets can't get through fences; he was trapped. Penned behind the fence, the runt tried not to feel sorry for himself, but the tree, for some reason, made him weep at his life as a runt.

Sobbing against a fence post, however, he realized that if he could climb the sty . . . . He wiped his eyes. Digging his tiny claws into the post and balancing paw by paw, he pulled himself clear to the top.

The view from the fence post sped his heart. Behind him, the wallow and sty looked drab . . . but familiar. Then the biggest piglet, who sat on him most often, yelled an insult with his mouth so full of grapefruit rinds that the runt could barely understand.

Rage overwhelmed the runt. He dug his claws into the fence post and climbed down the other side.

Alone on the ground he was, frankly, afraid. But the tree was still there, and he ran toward it. Its bark was deeply furrowed, and the runt discovered he could grab the ridges between the clefts and scamper up the tree as easily as he could run on flat ground. He just had to remember to hang on with some paws while he moved others.

The runt climbed the tree carefully and found the branch with the hollow he'd seen the creature run into. The creature was in the hollow.

"Excuse me," the runt said. "Is this yours?"

"Yes," the creature said. "But there's an empty on West 5."

"West 5?"

"Shall I show you?"

The runt was so surprised to be treated politely that he didn't answer immediately.

The creature leaned forward. "Might I ask you a personal question?"

Here it comes, the runt thought. It was too good to be true.

"Why did you stay with the pigs?" The creature paused. "Weren't you afraid of being trampled? We've all worried."

"Well, any runt has to stay alert."

"A runt?"

"The smallest piglet in a litter."

"Oh. We thought you were a squirrel."

"What's a squirrel?"

"*I* am," the squirrel replied.

The runt noticed the squirrel's paws and claws. He observed the squirrel's luxurious tail, then twisted sideways to see his own. He touched the squirrel's gray fur—specked white, beige at the throat, silky cool until his paw remained a moment and the fur felt like warm air. He could look the squirrel in the eye; he didn't have to talk up its snout.

The squirrel handed him an acorn. "Would you like to see West 5?"

The runt not only saw West 5; he moved into it. After a great deal of searching, he found his elderly mother, who recognized the distinctive blaze on his forehead and wept with gratitude that he was alive and well.

"Before your eyes opened," his ancient mother quavered, "you rolled out of our hollow. You were my liveliest—ever adventuring."

The story came out in clues and memories: Somehow, with the adaptability of the young, the fallen infant squirrel had wriggled toward warmth and found milk—and his role as the runt among piglets. He had, indeed, been alert and adventuresome to survive.

Among the squirrels, however, he found compatibility and friendship. Eventually, he even became a leader, admired for his understanding of a world beyond the squirrels'.

The
Lesson

A peasant needed a vacation. Onto his donkey he packed skis, poles, boots, a parka, waterproof map, goosedown quilt, two pumpkin pies, and a casserole. Leading his donkey toward the mountains on the horizon, the peasant passed through his village to see friends. However, while crossing The Old River Bridge in the center of town, the donkey lost its footing. The heavy pack of vacation gear slipped and threw the animal off balance, and the donkey fell into the river and drowned. The peasant, struggling to rescue the beast and save his possessions, perished beside his donkey.

The peasant and donkey were each buried honorably, but the villagers talked of nothing else. The blacksmith told anyone who entered his shop, "There's a lesson here for us all. Did you see that donkey's shoes? A few nails and four shreds of metal. The beast had no traction. Speaking no ill of the dead, now, that man signed his own death warrant, driving his animal on cobbled streets and a wooden bridge with worn-out shoes." Pumping his bellows as he spoke, the blacksmith, himself, swelled in importance.

The mayor saw the crowd gathering for the peasant's funeral, and shouted a challenge to the village council and his own constituents. Thrusting his arms out of his sleeves in his passion, he assailed the mourners. "How many lives must we sacrifice on this wretched pile of splinters my opponents call a bridge? I won't speak names on such a sad occasion. Simply let this loss galvanize—nay, inflame—us to build a new and better bridge to unite the two halves of our village. Out of pain, let purpose rise." The mayor dropped his arms to his sides and his voice to an anguished whisper. "Let us learn the lesson our departed citizen taught us: save on the bridge and spend on our funerals. May this man and beast not have died in vain."

An animal trainer in the crowd muttered to his wife, "The bridge wasn't the problem; the donkey was. You can't walk a country donkey through a thronging village on market day without problems. That animal wasn't people-proof, and there's your lesson."

Sunday at church, the minister gathered his flock to the sermon. "Friends," he intoned, "here is a lesson for each of us. Our neighbor who has left forever instead of just for a vacation, put his faith in an ass instead of the Lord, and the ass let him down. This unfortunate wanderer tried to make it through life on his own. He had not been in this building for so long that I cannot tell you now if his eyes were blue or brown. We are all wanderers, all on a voyage. But let us not put our faith in an ass."

The minister liked the topic so much he expanded it into three sermons, some of his best work. But two animal rights activists left the church permanently over the sermons. To them the peasant was a hero who gave his life trying to save a patient donkey. Their goal was to convince all peasants to load dray animals less heavily, and they felt the peasant's death taught the lesson that no animal can bear beyond its capacity. The peasant, they said, was a fool for overloading his donkey; but he was at least a brave fool who tried to save the animal when it foundered.

The peasant's partner in a hay-mowing venture disagreed with that noble assessment. "Greed," spat the partner from the corner of his mouth. "That was one wily peasant trying to save his material possessions. He was probably figuring the worth of the donkey, adding the value of the pack, and subtracting 25% for water damage, the second he gave up the ghost. He traded his life for his worldly belongings. Greed kills. That's the lesson; there is no other."

A fitness expert with a gym next door to the partner's office, smiled and shook his head. "Whether he drowned or dropped dead milking a cow, that peasant was a heart attack waiting to happen. Belly fat is lethal, and that man was loaded for a cardiac explosion. When his donkey slipped, he couldn't get out of the way. There's the lesson; that's the truth."

The peasant's wife wept more in fury than grief. "He was distracted by a guilty conscience," she said. "The idiot left me to finish the harvest—me with a new baby and the barn unroofed. He paid for his guilt, but I'm paying, too. There's justice, and then, again, there is none. That's the lesson."

The peasant's mother shook her head, pressing a handkerchief to her eyes. "A saint is gone from our midst. He was distracted—but by exhaustion. He worked his fingers to the bone and his back into a hump." The mother pointed her elbow at the peasant's wife. "Nothing was good enough. Nothing was enough, period. She drove him away; he fled his own land, his home, his baby, his mother. Learn his lesson before it's too late: get away from people who use you up! Save yourself! He was trying to, but he waited too long."

The villagers raised money to erect a statue of the drowned peasant and his donkey in the square where people would see them and learn from their example. Everyone contributed enthusiastically, and a noble equestrian statue was put up as soon as it was carved. But when it was time to inscribe its base, the villagers fell into such violent quarrels that they finally carved only the names of the peasant and donkey, and let each villager explain the real lesson to be learned from the drowning of the man and his beast.

The
Three
Wishes

nce upon a time a girl named Chlöe was
picking berries in the woods when she
came upon an old woman swooning beside a tree. Chlöe helped the crone regain her
senses by bringing her cool water in a folded leaf
and feeding her berries.

The old lady was so grateful for Chlöe's
kindness that she threw off her ragged cape
and revealed herself as a fairy godmother.
"Child, for your fine and generous spirit I hereby
grant you three wishes." She handed Chlöe
three small gold coins. "To make a wish, rub one
coin until it's warm and say out loud exactly what

you want. Use the coins wisely, dear, because when they're gone, they're gone forever." With that, the fairy godmother turned into a golden blaze, which rose into the sky and disappeared.

Chlöe put the coins into her bodice for safe keeping, and all afternoon while she picked berries she thought about what her wishes should be. At sundown her basket still wasn't full. But seeing all the berries on the bushes, she knew she'd never waste a wish to fill her basket.

Walking home, she noticed her torn, berry-stained dress. "I need a new one," she said. She imagined the dress she would wish for, in elegant satins and delicate silks, but what Chlöe needed was a dress for doing chores and going to school—something sturdy and comfortable, in a cheerful color, with pockets.

By the time she got home Chlöe had her dress all planned and was ready to wish for it. But as she held one of the gold coins, to rub it to make her wish, she remembered the fairy godmother's words: "Use them wisely, dear, because when they're gone, they're gone forever."

Chlöe looked from the magic coin in her hand to the dress in her mind and decided she could make the dress herself now that she knew what it looked like, and save her wish for something more difficult. But first she embroidered a delicate bag to hold her magic coins.

It took Chlöe a week to make the dress she saw in her mind, and her mother had to show her how to sew buttonholes; but the dress was just right. Chlöe wore it to school as soon as she finished it.

The first day Chlöe wore her dress, a new boy enrolled in school. He had agate eyes that turned to aquamarine when he spoke to Chlöe, and he was very smart. Chlöe considered using one of her coins to charm him, but realized how disastrous that would be if he turned out to be a smart but unpleasant person. She decided to know him better before using a coin.

The new boy, Norbert, was actually as friendly and warm as he was smart; he and Chlöe became best friends. Chlöe, convinced she could never find a finer friend than Norbert, decided to use her first gold coin to enchant him. At lunch that day, however, Norbert told Chlöe he loved her more than anyone else on earth and planned to cherish her forever. When he asked Chlöe if she adored him, she answered, "Absolutely," and saved her gold coin for another wish.

Chlöe grew up to be a weaver of extraordinarily fine tapestries in jewel colors. Norbert grew up to be a farmer, raising sheep, angora rabbits, and rare goats with long soft hair so Chlöe could spin the most exquisite yarns for her weaving.

One spring day Chlöe and Norbert married, in a dress and tuxedo Chlöe had woven and sewn, in a ceremony in the parlor of Norbert's farmhouse. It was lovely; everyone wept.

In their new house, with her looms and plump yarn balls, soup bubbling on the stove and pie puffing in the oven, Chlöe considered using a coin to wish she would always love Norbert as tenderly as she did at that moment. But she didn't see how she could not be devoted to someone as dear as Norbert, so she returned the gold coin to its embroidered bag until she needed it.

A year later Chlöe and Norbert had a baby daughter who had Norbert's eyes and Chlöe's chin. They named her Simone.

The most important gift Chlöe could give her baby was love, so she pulled a magic coin from the bag, to wish she would always love Simone. Just as Chlöe began rubbing the coin, warming it to make her wish, Simone looked up at her mother and smiled. Simone *glowed* when she smiled, and Chlöe dropped the coin back into its bag.

Simone's personality was as nice as her smile, and Chlöe and Norbert had two more babies, Henry and Belle. Chlöe tried to use a coin to love each of them, but just as she began to rub the coin, the baby would smile or coo, and Chlöe saved the coin for a time she would need it.

Once, when the babies were very sick, Chlöe got the coins to heal each of them, but she and Norbert thought they could nurse the children through this illness, and she didn't want to leave them without wishes for the rest of their lives. So they stayed up through the night, rocking the babies and cooling their fevers with sips of water and berry juice. In a few days the babies were well, and Chlöe still had her three wishes.

One winter a horrible blizzard threatened Norbert's goats and sheep. Chlöe knew a coin could melt the snow or stop the blizzard, but there would be more than two blizzards in future winters; she and Norbert needed to protect the animals permanently. So she left the coins in their embroidered bag while she, Norbert, and the children figured out ways to warm the animals.

They bundled baby animals on the hearth and huddled the big animals, to warm each other in the barn. They piled hay up the walls for insulation and let the goats and sheep eat it. The animals survived, and Chlöe and Norbert redesigned their barn for hot summers and blizzardy winters.

Chlöe wanted Norbert and the children to be healthy and strong; so she got out a coin to wish they would exercise, eat plain food, live calmly, and not smoke or drink. "We can do that ourselves," she said, returning the coin to its bag.

When the children grew big enough for school, Chlöe hoped they'd be brilliant and healthy, happy and good-looking, generous and friendly. But warming the first coin, she realized it was not her right to wish what Simone would become. Chlöe would have to leave a magic coin for Simone to make her own wish. Nor were Henry's or Belle's wishes hers to make, so Chlöe watched and listened as Simone, Henry, and Belle made their own choices.

The children grew up to choose careers and marry their favorites, leaving Chlöe and Norbert longer evenings to weave and tell stories.

Finally, Chlöe and Norbert grew very old.

Their friends were old, too; some had died. The farm was too big for them to run alone, and Chlöe wove on smaller looms with fatter yarn so she could see the designs. Chlöe asked Norbert if she should have wished them eternal youth. "No," he said. "We couldn't have traded away your weavings, my farm, or the children and grandchildren." So they just sat closer to the fire.

One sad evening Chlöe's beloved Norbert died. Chlöe knew she would die in her turn, if she didn't rub two magic coins and wish for them to live forever. She looked at Norbert, peaceful in his bed, and held a coin between her fingers. She formed the wish in her mind, "I wish Norbert would live forever . . . ." She stared at Norbert and at the room around her in the house where they would live in a world that was, in spite of their reading and listening and thinking, spinning slowly beyond their grasp. She slid the coin gently into the bag she had embroidered so delicately as a girl.

Years passed and Chlöe lay dying. Calling her children to her bedside, she gave each of them one gold coin to make the most important wish of their life.

The children had grown up knowing about the magic coins and finding ways to save them for things impossible to do themselves. Simone, Henry, and Belle each said, "Use my coin, Mama, and don't die."

"Thank you," Chlöe said. But she closed her eyes and wondered what heaven would be like with Norbert. "I've had the coins for a lifetime," she said. "They're yours now. Remember, dears, to save them for things you really can't do yourselves because when they're gone, they're gone forever."

And she didn't open her eyes.